KV-120-392

Cardiff Libraries
www.cardiff.gov.uk/libraries

Llyfrgelloedd Caerdy~
www.caerdyd.gov.uk~

CARDIFF

No CD 13/10/23
FW

ACC. No: 03216879

HORRiD HENRY'S
Sleepover

HORRiD HENRY'S
Sleepover

Francesca Simon
Illustrated by Tony Ross

Orion
Children's Books

Horrid Henry's Sleepover originally appeared
in *Horrid Henry's Stinkbomb*
first published by Orion Children's Books in 2002
This edition first published in Great Britain in 2014
by Orion Children's Books
a division of the Orion Publishing Group Ltd
Orion House
5 Upper Saint Martin's Lane
London WC2H 9EA
An Hachette UK Company
1 3 5 7 9 10 8 6 4 2

Text © Francesca Simon 2002, 2014
Illustrations © Tony Ross 2014

The right of Francesca Simon and Tony Ross to be identified
as author and illustrator of this work has been asserted.

All rights reserved. No part of this publication may be
reproduced, stored in a retrieval system, or transmitted,
in any form or by any means, electronic, mechanical,
photocopying, recording or otherwise, without the prior
permission of Orion Children's Books.

The Orion Publishing Group's policy is to use papers that
are natural, renewable and recyclable products and made
from wood grown in sustainable forests. The logging and
manufacturing processes are expected to conform to the
environmental regulations of the country of origin.

A catalogue record for this book is available from the British Library.

ISBN 978 1 4440 0003 0
Printed in China

www.orionbooks.co.uk
www.horridhenry.co.uk

There are many more **Horrid Henry** books available.
For a complete list visit
www.horridhenry.co.uk
or
www.orionbooks.co.uk

Contents

Chapter 1

Horrid Henry loved sleepovers.

Midnight feasts!

Pillow fights!

Screaming
and
shouting!

Rampaging till dawn.

The time he ate all the ice cream
at Greedy Graham's and left the
freezer door open!

The time he jumped on all the beds
at Dizzy Dave's and broke them all.

And that time at Rude Ralph's
when he – well, hmmn, perhaps
better not mention that.

There was just one problem.
No one would ever have
Horrid Henry at their house for
a sleepover more than once.

Whenever Henry went to sleep at a friend's house, Mum and Dad were sure to get a call at 3 a.m. from a demented parent screaming at them to pick up Henry immediately.

Horrid Henry couldn't understand it.
Parents were so fussy.
Even the parents of great kids like
Rude Ralph and Greedy Graham.

Who cares about a little noise?
Or a broken bed?
Big deal, thought Horrid Henry.

Chapter 2

It was no fun having friends
sleep over at *his* house.

There was no rampaging and feasting
at Henry's. It was lights out as usual
at nine o'clock, no talking,
no feasting, no fun.

So when New Nick, who had just joined Henry's class, invited Henry to stay the night, Horrid Henry couldn't believe his luck.

New beds to bounce on.
New biscuit tins to raid.
New places to rampage. Bliss!

Henry packed his sleepover bag
as fast as he could.
Mum came in. She looked grumpy.

"Got your pyjamas?" she asked.
Henry never needed pyjamas
at sleepovers because he never
went to bed.
"Got them," said Henry.
Just not *with* him, he thought.

"Don't forget your toothbrush,"
said Mum.
"I won't," said Horrid Henry.
He never *forgot* his toothbrush –
he just chose not to bring it.

Dad came in.
He looked even grumpier.
"Don't forget your comb," said Dad.
Henry looked at his bulging
backpack stuffed with toys
and comics.

Sadly, there was no room for a comb.
"I won't," lied Henry.

"I'm warning you, Henry,"
said Mum. "I want you to be
on best behaviour tonight."

"Of course," said Horrid Henry.

"I don't want any phone calls at three a.m. from Nick's parents," said Dad. "If I do, this will be your last sleepover ever. I mean it."

Nag nag nag.
"All right," said Horrid Henry.

Chapter 3

Ding dong.

Woof

Woof

Woof

Woof

Woof!

A woman opened the door.
She was wearing a Viking helmet
on her head and long flowing robes.
Behind her stood a man in a velvet
cloak holding back five enormous,
snarling black dogs.

"Tra La La
Boom-dy ay,"
boomed a dreadful,
ear-splitting voice.

"Brave, Bravo!" shouted
a chorus from the sitting room.

Grrrrrrr! growled the dogs.

Horrid Henry hesitated.
Did he have the right house?
Was New Nick an alien?

"Oh don't mind us, dear,
it's our opera club's karaoke night,"
trilled the Viking helmet.

"Nick!" bellowed the Cloak.
"Your friend is here."

Nick appeared. Henry was glad to see
he was not wearing a Viking helmet
or a velvet cloak.

"Hi, Henry," said New Nick.

"Hi, Nick," said Horrid Henry.

A little girl toddled over, sucking
her thumb.
"Henry, this is my sister, Lily,"
said Nick.

Lily gazed at Horrid Henry.
"I love you, Henwy,"
said Lisping Lily.
"Will you marry with me?"

"NO!" said Horrid Henry. Uggh.
What a revolting thought.

"Go away, Lily," said Nick.
Lily did not move.

"Come on, Nick, let's get out
of here," said Henry. No toddler
was going to spoil *his* fun.

Chapter 4

Now, what would he do first, raid the kitchen, or bounce on the beds?

"Let's raid the kitchen," said Henry.

"Great," said Nick.

"Got any good sweets?" asked Henry.

"Loads!" said New Nick.

Yeah! thought Horrid Henry.
His sleepover fun was beginning!

They sneaked into the kitchen.
The floor was covered with dog
blankets, overturned food bowls,
clumps of dog hair, and gnawed
dog bones. There were a few
suspicious looking puddles.
Henry hoped they were water.

"Here are the biscuits," said Nick.

Henry looked.
Were those dog hairs all over the jar?
"Uh, no thanks," said Henry.
"How about some sweets?"

"Sure," said Nick. "Help yourself."

He handed Henry a bar of chocolate.
Yummy! Henry was about to take a
big bite when he stopped.

Were those . . . teeth marks
in the corner?

"Raaa!"

A big black shape jumped on Henry,
knocked him down, and snatched
the chocolate.

Nick's dad burst in.
"Rigoletto! Give that back!"
said Nick's dad, yanking the
chocolate out of the dog's mouth.

"Sorry about that, Henry," he said,
offering it back to Henry.

"Uhh, maybe later," said Henry.

"Okay," said Nick's dad,
putting the slobbery chocolate back
in the cupboard.

Eeew, gross, thought Horrid Henry.

"I love you, Henwy,"
came a lisping voice behind him.

"Ah ha ha ha ha ha ha ha!"
warbled a high, piercing voice from
the sitting room.

Henry held his ears.
Would the windows shatter?

"Encore!"
shrieked the opera karaoke club.

"Will you marry with me?"
asked Lisping Lily.

"Let's get out of here,"
said Horrid Henry.

Chapter 5

Horrid Henry leapt on Nick's bed.

Yippee, thought Horrid Henry.
Time to get bouncing.

Bounce . . .

Crash!

The bed collapsed in a heap.

"What happened?" said Henry.
"I hardly did anything."

"Oh, I broke the bed ages ago,"
said Nick. "Dad said he was tired
of fixing it."

Rats, thought Henry.
What a lazy dad.

"How about a pillow fight?"
said Henry.

"No pillows," said Nick.
"The dogs chewed them."

Hmmn. They *could* sneak down and raid the freezer, but for some reason Henry didn't really want to go back into that kitchen.

"I know!" said Henry.
"Let's watch TV."

"Sure," said New Nick.

"Where is the TV?" said Henry.

"In the sitting room," said Nick.

"But – the karaoke," said Henry.
"Oh, they won't mind," said Nick.
"They're used to noise in this house."

Horrid Henry sat with his face pressed to the TV. He couldn't hear a word Mutant Max was shrieking with all that racket in the background.

"Maybe we should go to bed,"
said Horrid Henry, sighing.
Anything to get away from the noise.

"Okay," said New Nick.

Phew, thought Horrid Henry.
Peace at last.

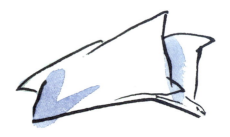

Chapter 6

Snore! Snore!

Horrid Henry turned over
in his sleeping bag and tried
to get comfortable.
He hated sleeping on the floor.

He hated sleeping with the window
open. He hated sleeping with the
radio on. And he hated sleeping
in the same room with someone
who snored.

Awhooooooo!
howled the winter
wind through the
open window.

Snore!
Snore!

"I'm just a lonesome cowboy, lookin' for a lonesome cowgirl," blared the radio.

Woof Woof
Woof
barked the dogs.

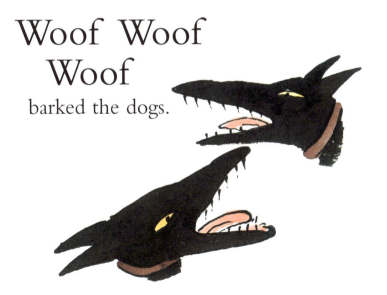

"Yeowwww!"

squealed Henry, as five wet,
smelly dogs pounced on him.

"Awhoooo!" howled the wind.

Snore! Snore!

"Toreador – on guard!"
boomed the opera karaoke
downstairs.

Horrid Henry loved noise.
But this was too much.
He'd have to find somewhere else
to sleep.
Horrid Henry flung open the
bedroom door.

"I love you, Henwy,"
said Lisping Lily.

Slam! Horrid Henry shut the
bedroom door.

Horrid Henry did not move.
Horrid Henry did not breathe.

Then he opened the door a fraction. "Will you marry with me, Henwy?"

Aaarrrgh!!!

Horrid Henry ran from the
bedroom and barricaded himself
in the linen cupboard. He settled
down on a pile of towels.
Phew. Safe at last.

"I want to give you a big kiss,
Henwy," came a little voice
beside him.

Nooooooo!

Chapter 7

It was three a.m.

"Tra la la boom-day!"

"—lonesome cowboy!"

Snore! Snore!

Awhooooooooooooooo!

Woof!
Woof! Woof!

Horrid Henry crept to the hall
phone and dialled his number.
Dad answered.
"I'm so sorry about Henry,
do you want us to come and get
him?" Dad mumbled.

"Yes," wailed Horrid Henry.
"I need my rest!"

What are you going to read next?

More adventures with Horrid Henry,

or go exploring with Shumba,

and brave the Jungle

and Arctic with Algy.

Find a frog prince with Tulsa

or even a big, yellow, whiskery

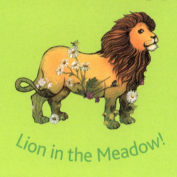

Lion in the Meadow!

Tuck into some

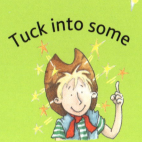

Blood and Guts and
Rats' Tail Pizza,

learn to dance with

Sophie,

travel back
in time with

Cudweed

and sail away in

Noah's Ark.

Enjoy all the Early Readers.

the orion star

Sign up for **the orion star** newsletter for all the latest children's book news, plus activity sheets, exclusive competitions, author interviews, pre-publication extracts and more.

www.orionbooks.co.uk/newsletters

Follow **O** @the_orionstar on **twitter**.

Orion
Children's Books

FW 8/14